SUN AND MOON

SUN
AND
MOON

by
NAOMI MITCHISON

Illustrated by
BARRY WILKINSON

THOMAS NELSON INC.
Nashville • Camden • New York

All rights reserved under International and Pan-American
Conventions. Published by Thomas Nelson Inc., Nashville,
Tennessee. Manufactured in the United States of America.

First U.S. edition

Library of Congress Cataloging in Publication Data

Mitchison, Naomi (Haldane)
    Sun and moon.

    SUMMARY: Recounts the adventures of Sun and
Moon, the twin children of Cleopatra and Mark Antony.
    [1. Egypt—History—332-30 B.C.—Fiction]
I. Wilkinson, Barry, illus.   II. Title.
PZ7.M699Su3   [Fic]   72-13012
ISBN 0-8407-6290-9

This book is dedicated to Dr. Mahmoud Manzalaoui of the University of Alexandria, with whom I explored today's city, and to E. M. Forster, who wrote the *Guide to Alexandria* many years ago, in the hope that he will approve my theory about how the lighthouse worked.

CONTENTS

Historical Note

The twins' mother is of course the Cleopatra about whom Plutarch wrote and Shakespeare after him. But remember that what we have heard is, much of it, Roman propaganda. The Romans were afraid of the Queen of Egypt and said hateful things about her and Mark Antony, her husband.

Cleopatra was the last of the Ptolemys, a long line of Macedonian kings and queens, descended from Ptolemy, Alexander's general. He was given Egypt to rule after Alexander died. But Cleopatra did speak Egyptian and she was a brave and clever leader, always thinking and planning for Egypt. She did have factories and trade monopolies and was particularly interested in trade with the east and with Africa to the south. At the time of this story, Octavian, who had declared himself Caesar's heir, was bent on destroying Antony and Cleopatra, since he could not bear the thought of another empire in the eastern Mediterranean.

For the story of Cleopatra in the carpet, you should read George Bernard Shaw's play *Caesar and Cleopatra*. Her lady-in-waiting, Charmian, who handed her the diadem in this story, can also be found in Plutarch and Shakespeare.

10

SUN AND MOON

The Twins

The twins lived in a little palace of their own, inside the great palace of Alexandria, where their mother, Queen Cleopatra of Egypt, lived and ruled. Their father, the great Roman general Mark Antony, came too when he could rest from the wars he had to fight.

The boy twin was called Alexander after Alexander the Great, who had ridden out from Macedonia and conquered the world and built the beautiful city of Alexandria where before there had only been a mud village at the mouth of the River Nile.

But Prince Alexander was also called Helios, which means "the Sun" in Greek. This was the

13

language they spoke with each other, though their mother the Queen also spoke in Egyptian to her subjects. They learned to read and write Greek, and Sun had to learn hundreds of lines of the old Greek poet Homer, who wrote about the siege of Troy.

The girl twin was called Cleopatra like her mother and many queens before her in the Macedonian line of kings and queens of Egypt, but she was also called Selene, which means "the Moon." When the moon was waning, Alexander used to point at it. "Look!" he'd say, "you're getting smaller; the big dragon has taken a bite out of you. You'll vanish!" His sister knew he was only teasing, but still she felt a little uneasy when the nights grew darker. Then she was happy again when the thin silver slip of the new moon showed in the velvet sky above the palace. Her moon.

When the sun slipped under a thundercloud

14

or dropped into the sea northwest of them, it was her turn to tease. "Oh, Sun, you'll be drowned, you'll be drowned!" Then she ran away before he could catch her and pull her long, moon-silky hair.

Sun and Moon were specially the children of Alexandria. Sometimes they were taken out onto the balconies to throw down sweets and nuts for the noisy crowds to scramble for. When their mother, Queen Cleopatra, came out herself, the shouting grew louder; people burst into songs in praise of her and started dancing with happiness. For it was she who fought and planned for Egypt, for Egypt's trade and prosperity. Above all, she was Queen of Alexandria.

What a splendid city! It had two big, safe harbors, for warships and merchant ships. It had markets and libraries and a gymnasium where people could play games or practice running and spear throwing. Sun went there with his tutor and already knew how to throw a light spear and do a good racing start.

There were baths and shady walks where people could meet and talk. And there was one thing more wonderful than all the rest. This was the Pharos, the huge lighthouse on the island beyond the harbors, towering far into the sky. On its top a bonfire was lit anew every evening, so that men could see it far out to sea and know there were a safe harbor and good markets in Alexandria.

But the twins at the palace had never been up there to see the great bonfire, and that was the one thing they most wanted to do. "It is the biggest magic in the world," Sun said to Moon. But his tutor, Theophilos, always said, "Later on, perhaps." And the head nurse, Madam Phaedra, who was a Greek from an old family and rather grand, simply said, "Prince

16

Alexander! Princess Selene! The idea!" and hustled them off to bed.

In front of the children's palace was a shallow pond, planted with lotuses and water lilies. It had striped and spotted fish in it. Moon liked feeding the fish and stopping the big, greedy ones from taking more than their share. This, she knew, was justice.

At her mother's Court of Justice, very poor people came, knowing that the great Queen would put things right. Sun and Moon sat on cushions at each side of their mother and sometimes when a very frightened peasant woman would come, hardly daring to whisper, Moon would smile at her and encourage her.

At the end their mother would explain things to them. For instance, there had been a man who had gotten into debt in a bad year when the harvest was poor. He had worked and worked. His neighbors and the priests at the temple of the goddess Isis had come to witness for him. But he had not been able to pay back the debt, and now the moneylender wanted to take his daughter, a little girl like Moon. "But you stopped him, Mother?" said Moon. She thought it had all ended well because the poor man had gone off looking happy.

"Yes," said Queen Cleopatra, "he had paid back all he had borrowed and more, but the moneylender had been greedy, so I gave judgment against him. That is not to happen in our land, my Moon."

Moon nodded gravely. This was being a Queen. But just then the ladies-in-waiting had come in to dress her mother for a banquet. "Please let me watch!" said Moon.

They smiled at her and began to prepare the Queen, sponging her with cool water and then putting on makeup around her eyes and a sweet shaping to her mouth. They dabbed her with scent from little stoppered earthenware bottles. They brushed her hair and curled it with tongs. The slave girls carried in dresses for her to choose from.

"Will you wear the crown, Mother? Oh, please wear the crown!" Moon looked across to where the treble crown of Egypt, strange-shaped, towering, protected by a golden serpent, stood by itself on a pillar of lapis lazuli.

Cleopatra laughed. "Not today, little Moon. That is the special crown for the time when I am Egypt, when my word is law. But this evening we'll all be gay. Your father will be there, and we'll have music. No, I'll wear a diadem." She reached out, and Charmian, one of her ladies-in-waiting, gave her a light wreath of golden leaves with flowers made of pearls and rubies. She put it on Moon, who stood very

19

straight and proud, and the slave girls stopped and clapped their hands.

But Sun liked playing with his father, the Roman general, who had had a suit of armor made specially for Sun. The body armor was solid gold and much too heavy, but Sun liked the helmet, which had a plume of ostrich feather, and he very much liked the sword. His father had shown him how to draw the sword and fight with it. He had shown him how one held the shield in the left hand and the sword in the right. The sword was sharp and real. Then one day he had fought with another boy, the son of one of the courtiers. He had cut him with the sword, and blood had dripped from the arm of this other boy. Sun had burst out crying. But his father had laughed.

It cost money to be a queen, to keep order, do justice, and be generous and hospitable. Queen Cleopatra had two or three factories close to the palace. Moon could never resist the weaving factory with the clicketing looms and the smell of the dye. She dodged her head nurses, and the younger nurses looked the other way because they knew where she was going and that they could find her quickly if they had to.

Moon would sidle in, and the slave girls standing at the looms, weaving fabrics for warm cloaks and rugs and blankets, all slowed down a little. They usually were kept hard at work, weaving and carding, but when Princess Moon came in there were smiles all around and the overseer's whip would be quiet.

What Moon really wanted was to get her arms into the dye vats, to push down the bundles of spun yarn that came out dripping scarlet, purple, blue, or yellow-green. "But what would your nurses say, Princess?" the overseer said, gently keeping her back. Yes,

Moon thought, what would they say! All too soon someone would run in and whisper that Madam Phaedra was on her way. Then Moon would dodge out by the other door, and if she was lucky she would get back to their own little garden and her own fishes without being seen.

The place Sun liked best was the racecourse. When his father, Mark Antony, came back from the wars, they would sit on a high seat beside the finish post, with Roman guards on each side, their swords drawn and looking very fierce. Sun and his father watched the light, bouncing chariots come around the bend. They each had one wheel off the ground as the charioteers yelled at one another and their horses and swung their whips and tore down the straight to the post. Oh, it was exciting! Best of all was when the leading charioteer wore their own favorite colors!

And how people cheered when Sun left the

racecourse, especially when he ran ahead of his father and the guards. He was their Prince, their Queen's son, the Lucky One. They even cheered his little brother Philo, when he was brought out onto a balcony by his special nurse.

Often Mark Antony, whose armies held half the world, was away from Egypt, leading his legions, his great sword flashing and his helmet crest tossing like the heroes in Homer's story of Troy. Sometimes his letters to Queen Cleopatra, his wife, took a long time to come, even when they were brought by messengers on galloping horses, and then given to other messengers on board fast boats which set their orange sails and caught the wind and came south to Alexandria, sailing night and day, until the captain saw the great Pharos, the lighthouse which all sailors knew—the lighthouse which Sun and Moon both wanted so very much to climb, right up to the very top!

2

"Me, Too!"

"Moon, Moon, come here!" It was Sun shouting as he charged into their own little palace from his lesson with Theophilos.

Moon had been having a lesson in harp playing, and her fingers were sore from the strings. Of course, when she was a grown-up princess, she would simply order the palace harp players to bring in their harps and play for her. But if she knew something about it, she would know if they were doing it right.

She would also learn the names of the different kinds of music, and at what time of day or night they should be played, and which could be mixed with flute music or cymbals or little

hand drums. Some kinds of music should be
played to visitors from far-off countries. An-

other kind should be played at a wedding or
when a baby was shown to his father for the
first time. A very solemn kind was for the
priests of Isis. But soldiers did not have harp
music; they had terrible bronze trumpets. And

shepherds called to one another across fields and canals with reed pipes.

Moon liked learning about all this from the harp players, an old man with white hair and two girls, who did most of the playing, sitting back on their heels on the floor. But what was Sun shouting about? "Go, my child," said the old man, "the Prince wishes for your presence."

"What is it now, Sun?" she said. He was waving his arms as if he were too excited to speak.

"You can't guess!" he said. "It is my reward. I learned so many lines of Homer, all about the siege of Troy, and I didn't get a word wrong!"

"But what is the reward?" Moon asked. "What? What?" And she jumped from one foot to the other.

"Guess!" said Sun and began jumping like his sister. "Guess!"

28

"You are to have a tame leopard with a gold collar," said Moon. "Or a monkey. Or a bird that talks."

"No," said Sun, "nothing like that!"

Moon thought hard. "I know, Sun! You will have your name cut on a marble pillar."

"No!" he said. "You're wrong, you're wrong!"

"Is it something to eat?" He shook his head. "Something to wear?" He shook his head again. "Well, then, it can't be anything nice!"

"I'll tell you," said Sun. "Theophilos is going to take me to the lighthouse. Tomorrow."

"Me, too!" said Moon. "Me, too!" And suddenly she was very nearly crying.

"Not you, Moon," said Sun. "Only me. Because I'm a boy. That's why."

Moon turned and ran into their own little palace. She had to get away. The rooms always

29

seemed full of people, like a beehive is full of
bees. She didn't want to be with any of them.
They wouldn't understand.

The head nurse of all, Madam Phaedra, always
wore a huge gold necklace, which clanked as
she walked, and dangling gold earrings. She
never did any real work herself, but ordered
the undernurses around. The next-to-head nurse
was an Egyptian lady called Madam Senobastis.
Her father was head priest at the temple of
Serapis, and Serapis was the special god of Alexandria and always had the best offerings. Senobastis wore Egyptian clothes, and her bracelets
were made like snakes. Her head was shaved,
but she wore a very large wig with two long
curls hanging down in front. She always spoke
in Egyptian to Moon, because it was the Queen's
orders that her children should grow up knowing both languages well. Their father spoke good

30

Greek, but he liked them to know a little Latin
and speak it with him.

Moon knew very well that Senobastis and
Phaedra didn't like one another. She always got
to know just how they were feeling, and sometimes she said and did things on purpose to make
them quarrel and look silly. Moon was fond of
the undernurses who dressed her and brushed
her hair and played games with her and told her
riddles and rhymes. Only she didn't much like
Leontion, who was Phaedra's daughter. She was
dreadfully stuck up and tattle tale and tried to
order people around.

But Moon didn't speak to any of the nurses
about the lighthouse. She knew what they
would all say. Her little brother Philo was playing with a toy horse and cart. One of the nurses
was bringing him shiny pebbles; he loaded them
onto the cart and pretended to beat the horses.

31

He was a boy. When he was older, he would be taken to the lighthouse, just because he was a boy.

Everywhere, thought Moon, boys did interesting things. Poor boys helped their fathers to make boats and carts and drove the oxen around to step out the grain or lift water from the canals. They went out with the fishing boats. They climbed trees for fruit. They scared the birds off the crops and shot them with bows and arrows. They dived into the river Nile and swam right across.

But their sisters could only carry water and card wool, and every day for hours and hours grind grain for flour or pound seeds for oil. Well, water carrying was difficult and fun. Moon knew how to carry a pot on her head. One of the undernurses had shown her. They had all run races carrying milk pots on their heads and laughing.

32

What was she to do now? She would try
once more. She went out again. "Sun," she said,
"can't I come to the lighthouse? Oh, I do so
want to come!"

"No," said Sun, "this is just for me. It is the
Pharos of Alexandria. It is · special. They
wouldn't let you come. You know that, Moon."

"Ask Theophilos, Sun. Ask him!"

"Even if he did, Phaedra wouldn't let you
come. Besides—Moon, I *did* ask."

"Oh. Well, then—I don't know." But Sun
had asked. So that wasn't so bad. Only now
she'd have to think. To think like a princess.
Phaedra and Senobastis both looked at her in
an interested way. They thought she was going
to ask them. Then they'd say No. Both of them
would look pleased saying No. So she wasn't
going to speak.

Evening came. There were lights in the great
palace of Queen Cleopatra. In rooms and pas-

sages, lamps burned oil that gave a clear, sweet-smelling flame. Outside there were torches stuck into rings on the walls, smoky and flaring. The palace guards put in fresh ones whenever they burned down. Sounds of singing or music floated down from lighted halls, and high above all, the stars hung in the velvet-dark sky. But always to the north there was the strong glare of the lighthouse.

In the children's small palace the nurses put Philo to bed with his toys all around him, singing softly to him until he slept. Then it was the turn of the twins. Sun went to sleep almost at once, but Moon lay awake. Then came what she was waiting for, a square of cool light on the marble of the floor. She got up and went and stood in it, looking up and out at the almost-full, floating moon. Princess Selene looked the moon full in the face and whispered to it, "Help me. Show me a way. You have to help. You are me."

34

One of the younger nurses, tiptoeing around
to see that all was well, saw Moon speaking to
the moon. She crept away, a little afraid.

3

The Lighthouse

Sun ran out and past the fish pond. He was going to the lighthouse at last. He had not wanted to see Moon or to hear her say anything. His own special nurse had put in the shoulder brooches of his best tunic, the finest wool dyed reddish-purple with dye from a kind of mussel, and edged with gold—real gold beaten into the finest possible thread to embroider the wool. His belt was gold with a ruby set in the clasp, and there were two rubies on the gold buckles on his sandals.

Going to the lighthouse, oh, going to the lighthouse! But he had dropped his riding cloak, and the nurse had to come running after him and put it over his shoulders just as he got to the horses. The other young nurses all ran out too, and waved to him.

He had a white mare called Snowstorm who was gentle and didn't shy when people shouted. Mark Antony had given her to Sun, telling him about white snowstorms in the Alps and the Thracian mountains. Snowstorm was not a very tall horse, but she seemed tall to Sun, who started, as he had been taught, by patting Snowstorm's nose and letting her smell his hand.

"Now we mount, Prince!" said Theophilos. He was riding a mule with a silver-tasseled bridle. Two of the grooms came forward, holding their hands together as an extra step for Sun on his way up to the saddle. Snowstorm turned her neck a little and cocked one ear back to make sure that the light weight was really safe on her back. The grooms mounted. Sun thought proudly that last year he'd had to have a leading rein, but now he didn't need one any longer.

38

He had been up on the front of his father's
saddle on Mark Antony's great black charger,
North Wind, and had felt the tremendous body
under him heaving into a quick, shaking trot
and then into a canter. But all the time he had
his father's arm tight around him keeping him
safe. Now he was alone. He gathered up his

reins like a man and sat straight. Was Moon looking on? He didn't know. He didn't want to see.

They went through the gate of the palace, which was flung open wide for him, and onto the straight paved road that crossed Alexandria from end to end. There were shaded walks at each side of the great street. Stone columns faced the traffic, and shop fronts were full of all the things which people bought and sold in Alexandria.

There were shoes and cloaks and rugs and belts. There was beautiful silk which had been brought thousands of miles from China and was very expensive, but the court ladies always wanted it. There were metal pots, swords and knives and shields, jewelry and gold work, harps and flutes, food and dye stuffs, fruit, sweets, cage birds, slaves, lamps, drinking cups, flowers, fish, scent, and medicine—anything and everything.

40

At the sides of the road there were always letter writers, wearing their old-fashioned wigs and sitting waiting so that people who couldn't read or write could get letters written for them. Other people were getting shaves or haircuts or having their fortunes told. But everyone stopped and looked up and waved or called out when Prince Alexander rode by so shiningly on his white horse.

Past the end of the palace they turned north toward the harbor and the long causeway that had been built out across the shallows to join the mainland to Pharos Island. On one side was the harbor for fishing boats; on the other side there were warships and merchant ships. The warships had great bronze-sheathed beaks on them to ram into other ships and long oars with three men to each for quick rowing.

One of the merchant ships was being loaded with barley. A string of donkeys was being driven along one side of the causeway, carrying baskets. They trotted back quickly on the other side with the baskets empty, with the boy who had been driving them up on top with his bare legs dangling. Another ship was still being unloaded. It had come from the north, bringing hides and furs. The bales were being hauled up out of the hold and smelled terrible. Snowstorm tossed her head and Sun got her to trot, but not very fast because the top of the causeway was paved with stone.

At the other side, most of the fishing boats were away, but one or two were being mended or tarred or had new rigging being fitted. One day, thought Sun, he would go out in a fishing boat, and they would let him cast the clever net that flew out in a circle and dropped over the fish and was then drawn tight.

On the island itself the road took them through fishing villages with the women busy in their little houses. Everywhere people recog-

42

nised him and ran out and cheered. But Sun was looking ahead at the Pharos, the great tower of the lighthouse. It seemed to get bigger and bigger, so big he was almost afraid. From time to time they passed strings of donkeys going slowly, with loads of wood across their backs.

They were coming close. There was a square courtyard at the bottom with pillars and a shaded walk all around. The lighthouse rose from its middle. In the corners there were huge piles of wood. The tired donkeys rested with their heads down till they were driven back for another load. The bottom story was square, with a huge doorway in it. Here the engineers and servants lived and the spare parts were kept.

Sun watched them bringing the wood in through the huge door and piling it onto a platform at the end of an enormous chain that went up, up and over a pulley right at the top of the tower. They showed him a huge caldron at the

43

other end of the chain and explained that it was filled with water. The weight of that pulled the wood to the top. Then the wood was unloaded. But how was the platform brought down for another load? By letting out all the water in the caldron into a tank. Then the caldron end went up and the platform end came down.

"How do you get the water back into the caldron?" said Sun.

"Well, here it is in the tank at the bottom," said one of the engineers. "But we twist it up to another tank with this Archimedes screw— look, Prince—and from there to a still higher tank by another screw, and so on, till we get it into the top tank. Then we drain it into the caldron again as soon as they shout from the bottom that they are ready with their load. See?"

There were slaves, working in shifts, to turn the great screws that pulled the water up. Half

a day's work would pull up enough wood to keep the fire alight for a night on the top of the tower. Sun listened, but found it difficult to understand. His tutor asked most of the questions.

In the square block of building, a staircase led up, going around the dark well of the pulley and chains. Sun didn't much care for all those gloomy steps, but up he went bravely. Snow-storm stayed in the courtyard, but not with the donkeys. Here and there doors led off to store-rooms or workshops. At last he got out onto a platform with a railing around it.

Now he was as high as the great hall of the palace with the balconies that looked out over the harbor. He ran from one side to the other. But he must go on and up another staircase in the eight-sided second story. This came out on another, narrower platform, and now he could see right over the roofs of the great palace and south beyond the city to the green plain. Yes, there was their own little palace and the fish pond aglitter in the sun! Was Moon down there?

The next story was circular, somewhat smaller, and the stair still wound around the clanking well where the chain went steadily up and down. When they came out at the top, there was only a very narrow platform, and Sun didn't at all mind when Theophilos held his hand. But now he could see the many-mouthed river Nile winding away to the south. He could see over the hump of the island and away out to sea.

And here, on a special platform, was the fire laid, ready to light when dusk came. There were piles of wood at each side, but far enough away for no accident to happen. Behind it, on the landward side, were great curved sheets of silver. "Explain!" said Sun.

48

The engineer in charge began to explain to Sun that these sheets of polished silver reflected the light of the fire, each one making the light twice as bright; and not only that, but they reflected the fire back and forth, one to another. "Look, Prince, we can adjust the mirrors." They were in frames which moved, and the engineer showed how they could be tilted this way and that to catch the flame at its brightest. "The fire must be fed very carefully," said the engineer, "so that the flames stay in the center."

"Do you do it?"

"Yes, Prince. But there are always two of us here every night from dusk to dawn. We make our prayer to Poseidon and then we stay busy."

"What's that?" said Sun suddenly, pointing to a big bronze tube.

"Ah, that," said the engineer. "You will see, Prince. Look out beyond the island. What is there?"

49

"Three fishing boats—isn't it?"

"Now, I point the tube at them. Look through it, Prince."

Sun put his eye against the end of the tube and then squeaked with excitement, "But

50

they're big! I can see men on them! I can see the sails! Oh, they've come closer!"

But they hadn't. It was only when he looked through the tube that they were big. Theophilos looked too, and was just as excited. "It's quite simple really, Prince," said the engineer. "There is a lens in the tube. When you look through it, it makes everything bigger."

"Why?"

"It is the nature of the lens, Prince Alexander," said Theophilos, who had studied mathematics. But that didn't help.

"It's magic," said Sun happily.

4

The Pot of Milk

"Where is the Princess?" asked Madam Phaedra in a loud and angry voice.

One of the undernurses said timidly, "When Prince Alexander left us to go to the lighthouse, she lay down on her bed and held the cover over her head."

"She should have been amused—taken out of herself! You are a pack of frightened fools!" Madam Phaedra glared at them. "Find her! At once!"

Senobastis came gliding in. "What is this? The Princess has disappeared? How could this have happened?"

Madam Phaedra said, "Prince Alexander should never have been allowed to go to this stupid lighthouse. But his tutor does these things behind my back!"

"And mine," said Senobastis. For once they were in agreement. "Well, she can't be far off."

But she was. True enough, she had run to her bed and thrown herself down. She wasn't going to let Sun see how she cared! But then, when all the nurses were seeing Sun off and admiring him and waving to him, she had her idea. She ran quickly the other way, dodging behind columns and statues and flowering peach trees, toward the great palace kitchens. The idea began to get better, or perhaps big sister moon in the sky, whose help she had asked last night, was whispering to her.

Then suddenly, around a corner, there was Leontion, Phaedra's daughter. She caught

54

Moon by the hand. "Where are you going so fast, Princess?" she asked.

"Let go!" said Moon, but Leontion didn't let go.

Moon stopped pulling, but she spoke in a different way, not angry but cold. "I am the Princess," she said. "You are nothing. Do not touch me."

Leontion was so surprised that she let Moon go. Moon looked at her and said, "If you tell your mother this, it will be a mark against you for always. When I am not a child any longer." She went away quietly, and Leontion looked after her with her hands up to her mouth, suddenly afraid of Queen Cleopatra's daughter and not knowing what to do.

Moon was in a very dark passage near the kitchens when she saw what she wanted—one of the maids, only a little older than she was, carrying a pot of milk on her head. The girl was wrapped in a brown cloak. It was just a piece of coarse, undyed stuff around her and over her head, torn at the edges.

"Stop!" said Moon. The girl trembled and went down on her knees. She knew it was the Princess. Moon took the pot of milk and put it on the ground. "Now," she said, "I want your cloak." The girl was too scared to move, so Moon pulled it off and wrapped herself in it. Then she picked up the pot of milk and put it on her head.

The girl, who was only wearing a short, dirty tunic under the cloak, began to cry and pointed at the milk. "They will beat me," she whispered.

Moon had a thin gold bracelet on her wrist. She pulled it off. "That pays for the beating," she said, "and the cloak." And indeed it would! The girl took it, staring at Moon with grateful eyes, and hid it under her tunic. "Now," said

56

Moon, "not a word!" The girl nodded. Moon held the edge of the cloak across her face. It smelled like goats. "Am I like you?" she asked.

Now the girl began to giggle a little, shook her head, and pointed at Moon's sandals showing under the cloak. They were made of soft white leather with little golden leaves sewn on them here and there. They didn't go with the cloak and the milk pot. Moon kicked them off into a corner. "Now open the door for me," she said.

"Oh, Princess, your Highness," the girl said, "you must not go out alone!"

"But I must. I order you to let me out. Go on. I order you!"

What could the girl do? She had to obey the Princess, the Queen's daughter. She led Moon to a small door and unbarred it, for it was too high for Moon to reach. She prayed to Egypt's goddess Isis that all would be well. The Princess

58

had said to her, "Not a word." She must not speak. And she would be beaten for the lost milk and cloak. She began to make up a story about it. But the bracelet! She felt it with her fingers. She would hide it deep in her straw mattress. Not one of the other kitchen girls had a golden bracelet or was ever likely to. Oh, she was lucky!

Moon trotted, balancing the milk pot on her head, going along the palace wall. She didn't mind going barefoot unless she came to a very dirty place. She knew she must get to the cause-way. It would be best to take the big street, where there was always such a crowd that no-body would notice one more little girl in a dirty old cloak, carrying a pot on her head. Oh, thought Moon, what fun to be just an ordinary, barefoot little girl, to dodge out of the way instead of having the way cleared! And what fun the street was, when one was close to the shops and the fortune-tellers and the boys with fighting cocks and the performing monkeys!

She almost stopped at one of the sweet shops where they were spinning out threads of honey and crushed nuts to bake on hot iron plates over a charcoal fire. But then she remembered she had no money. She couldn't say she was the Princess and demand that the shopkeeper give her some, or she would be caught. So on she went trotting to the crossroads down to the causeway.

But back at the palace, more and more people were looking for her. Madam Phaedra and Senobastis rushed around like whirlwinds. Boys jumped into all the ponds and felt among the lily leaves in case she had fallen in. Everyone asked everyone else. But nobody yet had told Queen Cleopatra. Madam Phaedra was planning how she could lay the blame on Senobastis, but

Senobastis was sure she could lay it on Madam Phaedra.

They had looked in all the corners. Phaedra had a switch in her hand, and every time she saw one of the undernurses she gave her a cut with it to keep her on the move. She saw her daughter Leontion, but Leontion was too frightened to speak. How can one be frightened of a girl child? But if the child speaks in that cold voice, it is very frightening. She will be like the Queen, her mother, Leontion thought, and nobody will dare to disobey her.

Then one of the nurses came running with the sandals, which had been found in the long passage leading to the kitchens. Phaedra rushed down there and began questioning the cooks, but nobody knew anything. There was a girl crying in the corner because she had been whipped. She looked at them through her fingers. Nobody bothered to question her, but if

61

they had, she would have said nothing. And the bracelet was still there hidden in her mattress, so the whipping didn't matter.

"We shall have to tell the Queen," said Madam Phaedra, more and more anxious and angry.

"*You* will have to tell the Queen," said Senobastis.

5

The Message

A little girl with a pot of milk on her head was trotting along the causeway, sometimes stopping to look at the boats, but hurrying on if anyone shouted at her. She was beginning to get rather tired and very hot. She had knocked her toes on the mooring rope of one of the merchant ships and almost dropped her pot of milk. After that she walked more slowly.

It wasn't such fun now. She thought they must have noticed by this time at the palace that she had gone. But she wouldn't let them catch her, no! Every now and then she looked back over her shoulder. And she was tired, tired. The hot stones were burning her feet.

She sat down for a minute on a big stone and looked at the pot of milk. The other, ordinary little girl she had turned into just had to take her milk pot to the lighthouse.

For there it was, still a long way off, and so

big! She turned to the right on the island and came to a fishermen's village. She was so used to people running out and cheering and singing welcoming songs wherever she went that for a moment she wondered why they didn't.

Then at the corner a crowd of boys ran at her. They were only little boys, most of them wearing nothing but rags around their middles, but they were singing an altogether different kind of song, a very nasty song that said, "Stranger, get out!" It went on to say, "Stranger with the ugly face, Stranger with the dirty feet, Stranger with no nose, Stranger with devils on your back, Stranger smelling like old fish"— And always, "Get out, get out!"

She backed against a wall and they all stood around and sang at her and made ugly faces, and some of them threw little stones and sharp shells. One of them poked her with a stick. Her hand was grazed and bleeding red drops. Should she pull the cloak off and show herself? But would they know her? She was nearly crying. Then she was really crying.

But at last a woman came out of one of the houses and shouted at the boys. They scattered with a few last whistles, and one of them threw a clod of earth that she couldn't quite dodge. The woman said nothing to her, not one word. So it's like that, thought Moon, not to be a princess.

Beyond the village there were not many people. The lighthouse was getting nearer, the place where she'd wanted so much to go. But did she now? Her feet hurt. Her hand hurt. There was so little shade, and not one cloud between her and the sun. She stood back for a string of donkeys to pass. No, she must go on.

She reached the lighthouse at last and the square high wall round the courtyard. If she walked straight in as though she knew her way or had a message, they wouldn't stop her. And there was Snowstorm, Sun's horse! He must be here. Lucky Sun, who hadn't had to walk. And now she must see him, she must show him!

And then a man was standing in front of her, a man with a short black beard and angry dark eyes. He was wearing a good, embroidered tunic with a gold amulet hanging around his neck. "What are you doing here, little girl?" he asked.

Moon thought quickly. "I have come with a message for Prince Alexander," she said.

"Nonsense," said the man. And yet, he thought to himself, the child speaks out and she has a sweet voice. He himself was an engineer, one of the men who understood the mirrors and the magic tube. He looked at her. A message for the Prince? Could they possibly have sent a messenger like this? "Who do you say this message is from?" he went on.

"From his mother, the Queen," said the little girl, looking at him with steady eyes.

"Where is it then?" asked the engineer.

"It is a secret message," said the little girl and she pointed to the pot of milk.

Perhaps this is a trick, the engineer thought, by some enemy. The milk is poisoned! Or there could be a serpent hidden in it. "You are lying," he said. "I'll have you whipped."

"You had better not," said the little girl.

The engineer didn't know what to think. The child might be lying, or she might be mad. It might be a plot against the Prince. Or else, of course, she might really have been sent by the Queen, to test him. It was the kind of extraordinary thing that Queen Cleopatra might do. "Does the Prince know you?" he asked. The little girl nodded. "Very well," he said, "I will take you to him. But not near. And then you must empty out your milk on the floor."

69

"I will do that," she said. "Now, please take me. And tell me what is happening in there." She pointed to the great opening and the wood being carried in all the time.

The engineer found himself explaining a lot of things to the little girl as they went up. She still had the milk pot on her head. Why was he doing this for a child in a dirty old cloak? He didn't know. He only knew that she was fearless. She understood about the pulley and partly understood about the water caldron that outweighed the load of wood. And she asked questions which showed that she knew who had built the lighthouse and when. She could even read the letters of the inscriptions.

And then at last they were coming up to the very top, to the lantern where the fire was laid. They could hear the voices of the Prince and his tutor. And now the little girl was smiling and beginning to run up the last steps. He put out

70

his hand and stopped her. She must do as he said and throw down the milk in case it was poisoned.

"Now!" he said. "Throw the milk down and we'll see what the message is!" She did and there was nothing in the pot, nothing but milk. The Prince looked up without taking much notice. He was still looking through the tube and was too interested to turn around.

But then the little girl dropped the dirty old cloak and the engineer saw that she had a delicate dress of embroidered linen and a moonstone on a chain around her neck. He saw the moon-silky hair, which had been hidden under the cloak. "Moon!" said Sun and rushed to hug her. "Oh, there's such a lot to see!"

"Princess Selene!" said Theophilos. "What is this? How did you get here?"

But the engineer, remembering that he had threatened to whip her, fell on his knees.

6

The Magic Tube

Sun was explaining everything to Moon. They
ran to the great window spaces opposite the
mirrors and looked out, far out to sea. Away
over there were the countries they'd heard
about—Persia, Athens, where everyone had
welcomed their father, Rhodes, Crete, Cilicia,
Macedonia, from which their own ancestors had
come. And Rome, where their father's enemies
were. But below them, past the balconies, they
could see part of the courtyard.

"Look, there's Snowstorm," said Sun. "You
shall ride her back." Then he had to know ex-
actly how she had come. He laughed and
laughed. "They'll be so angry," he said.
"They'll burst!" But Theophilos knew that

Madam Phaedra would somehow try to throw the blame on him, and he felt rather uneasy.

But the black-bearded engineer felt worse. At last Moon was standing still, making faces at the great silver mirrors that reflected them all but made them look such curious shapes because they were curved. The engineer kissed her bare feet. "Does the Princess forgive her servant?" he asked anxiously.

"No!" she said, just to see what he'd look like, but he looked so sad that she began laughing. "Yes, I do," she said, "but you must never, never try to whip little girls, because you never know—they may be princesses!" And she gave him her hand to kiss instead of her toes.

"You haven't seen the magic tube yet," said Sun. "Can I show her?" And they looked at all the boats in sight, while the engineers adjusted it and did things with screws and tried to explain how it worked. "There is only one in the world," said Sun.

"And that's in Alexandria," said Moon, "of course!" Then she looked out of the other window, to the west, and there was the causeway which had been such a long, long hot walk. But it was tiny and the donkeys looked like ants, and you could see down, down into the water, yellowish where it was sandy and shallow, and darker where it was deep and the war galleys lay. But what was that at the end of the causeway?

"It's the hounds!" said Sun, excited. "They gave them something of yours to smell and they're tracking you."

"But they won't eat me?" said Moon, suddenly scared.

"Of course not," said Sun. "We men will protect you."

"I wonder who else is coming," said Moon, worried.

"That's something we shall be able to see," said the engineer, who had shown Sun the tube,

and he carefully carried it, on its stand, which was made like a kneeling man of bronze with his arms up. Then he pointed it down toward the people. "Now look," he said.

The twins both looked and then nodded to one another. Then Theophilos looked. "Madam Phaedra and Madam Senobastis!" he said. "I am afraid they'll be very angry." He shook his head. "My dear Princess, you have got us all into trouble."

Moon seized hold of the black-bearded engineer. "You'll protect me—won't you?"

"To the death, Princess," he said, "but it will not be necessary. I shall go down now and stop them bringing the hounds into the courtyard. They would disturb the donkeys." He turned and ran down the stairs, while the hounds and the men who kept them on their leads, and the nurses and the undernurses, and quite a lot of other people came streaming across the island.

The children looked at them through the magic tube until they got too near for it to be able to point down at them. They could hear, very faintly, the baying noise of the hounds coming up from below.

"I can't have everyone in here," said the chief engineer. "They would upset things. Especially those women. We will go down and meet them."

"Must I?" said Moon.

"It will be more dignified, Princess," said Theophilos, "so I advise you to do so."

"One more peep!" she said.

"But we'll come again," said Sun. "Often. Both of us."

They went down to the first balcony, the broad one above the square block of the first story. It would be the best place to face the head nurses. But if Madam Phaedra is against us, thought Theophilos, Senobastis may be for us.

Luckily Madam Phaedra was somewhat out of breath by the time she was at the top of the winding steps. But she started at once, "Princess Selene, I am ashamed of you! You have betrayed your friends and protectors. You have given us all so much pain and anxiety. You have behaved most wickedly. The gods will certainly punish you!"

Poor Moon didn't know what to say. But by this time Theophilos had decided he must speak. "Nobody has been hurt, Madam Phaedra, except our little Princess herself, whose feet are sore from her long walk. And she has had a most educative time at the lighthouse. Yes, it has all been for the best."

Then they started arguing with one another, getting more and more angry and speaking in louder voices. Senobastis, who had come up behind Phaedra, did not join in, but instead came around and stroked Moon's hair. Moon didn't really want to be stroked, but it couldn't be helped. She knew it was done to annoy Phaedra. She said to Senobastis, "I have found many good friends," and waved her hand at the two engineers. The one with the black beard was now finding it all rather funny.

"Come on!" said Sun. "We'll go down and find Snowstorm." They stole off past the argument and down the steps, with the black-bearded engineer, who suddenly stooped and picked up Moon's old cloak. "You will not want this any longer, Princess?"

"No," she said, "it smells of goats. I don't want that and I don't want my milk pot, and the milk is spilled."

"Princess," said Black Beard, "have I your leave to keep the cloak and the milk pot? I would like to tell my own daughters the story of Princess Selene."

"Of course you can keep them," said Moon.

80

"How old are your little girls?"

"Younger than you, Princess," said the engineer, "but I hope they will grow up as brave as you are."

That was nice for Moon to hear. Now she and Sun could go and see the hounds which had traced her. They were large, lolloping, heavy-jawed beasts, but quite friendly. Only then they heard the others all coming down the stairs, still arguing. "I shall take her straight to her mother the Queen," said Madam Phaedra to Theophilos, "and we shall see what she says to all your excuses." Then she took Moon very hard by the hand and said, "She will punish you, Princess Selene, I can promise you that! She will be angry, very angry!"

"But perhaps she will be most angry," said Senobastis to Theophilos, "with certain people who might have been taking better care of the Princess."

The Queen in Judgment

Queen Cleopatra of Egypt did not very much wish to see the head nurses just then. She was with the Treasurer and his scribes. They were trying to see what help she would be able to send to her husband Mark Antony, who was away preparing for war. She must send him warships and also regular shiploads of grain for his soldiers. But how much grain could be spared? How much wheat? How much barley? Perhaps, too, he would need woolen cloth for his soldiers next winter. As for gold itself, she and the Treasurer together must decide about that, too.

However, she said the nurses could come, and

in rushed Madam Phaedra, who did most of the talking, telling the Queen how Princess Selene had deliberately disobeyed her and run away. It was ridiculous, of course, and ill judged, to take either of the children to see the lighthouse. Here she turned and glared at Theophilos, who had followed the nurses in. He pursed his lips and looked down his nose.

However, said Phaedra, in the case of Prince Alexander, it had been done without consulting her. But the Princess had been told she could not go. Phaedra shook her head accusingly. "She is self-willed and she would not listen. She has betrayed the trust her guardians put in her. She must be punished."

"But why did no one see?" asked the Queen.

"Yes, yes," said Senobastis, "that was what I asked myself. Unhappily I was not on duty."

Madam Phaedra gave a nasty look at Senobastis. But the Queen must be answered. "The

84

Princess pretended to be upset when her brother left the palace. We all respected this. But she was sly. She slipped away somehow. We do not yet know how she got out of the palace. The Queen herself must question her. She will not answer me. After I have been her nurse all these years! It saddens me."

"Very well," said Cleopatra, "bring in the Princess."

Sun and Moon came in together, with as many of the under-nurses as could squeeze in after them, and now Moon was crying. She was frightened, much more frightened than she had been when the boys in the fishing village attacked her. "Come, Moon," said Queen Cleopatra. "No, not you, Sun. Come here, Moon, and tell me what you did that has so upset your poor head nurse."

Moon came slowly over. She didn't feel at all sorry for Madam Phaedra. She opened her

mouth stickily and said, rather too loudly, "I
had to go to the lighthouse!"

"You see, Your Majesty," said Phaedra, "she
had been told she must not go and she simply
disobeyed me!"

"Yes, yes," said Cleopatra, "I know all that.
Come nearer, Moon." She began to wipe
Moon's face with the edge of her own beautiful
silken skirt. "And so you had to go. But how
did you get out of the palace and where did you
get the old cloak and the milk pot?"

Moon went on crying. "I don't know," she
said and stuck her thumb into her mouth.

"I think you do know," said the Queen, who
had so often sat in judgment, "but you will not
tell. I think that is because you are afraid, if you
did tell, that the one who helped you would be
punished. Is that it?" Moon nodded hard, but
kept her thumb in her mouth. "But all the same
that person should not have done it."

87

"She must be found and punished!" said Phaedra.

"What do you think of that, Moon? She put you into danger. Doesn't that mean she should be punished?"

"I made her do it!" said Moon and took her thumb out. "I am the Princess. I ordered her."

"Well, well," said her mother, "so it was not her fault, whoever she was. I see. No, keep quiet, Phaedra! I am judging this. And then you ran barefoot across Alexandria with a milk pot on your head. It is as well I have a peaceful and orderly city." She pulled Moon a little nearer and then picked up her grazed hand. "But what is this? Did someone try to hurt you?" She frowned.

"It was only some boys," said Moon.

"Tell me where. This is not to happen. I shall hang them all on a high gallows."

"No," said Moon. "No, please! They were only silly, horrid little boys! They didn't know. I wasn't really hurt. No, Mother, no! Stop being angry, Mother!"

"You want mercy for them? Very well, you are my wise daughter. But it shall be known. And when you got out to the Pharos?"

Moon had stopped crying, but she thought she wouldn't say too much about the black-bearded engineer, "Well, I said I had a message for Sun and I made it sound important, and I went up and I saw the mirrors and the place for the fire and the clanking chain and the donkeys and everything. And, oh, Mother, there is a magic tube and when you look in it, everything is big! And it is so high, so very high! One can see the whole world."

"Did you understand how the mirrors worked? Sun, did you understand?"

"I think we ought to go back at night, both of us, and see it lit up," said Sun, "then I think we would understand."

"Do you indeed! But it is one of the wonders of the world. It should make you proud that all was thought of and made here in Alexandria."

"I *am* proud," said Moon, and now she was leaning close up to her mother.

"Phaedra and Senobastis, you may go," said Queen Cleopatra. "Theophilos, you may go, but you must try to explain the mathematics of all this to the children. Especially that magic tube."

"But her disobedience—" said Madam Phaedra. "Her punishment—"

"Phaedra," said the Queen, "I said you could go. Later on, I shall consider who is to be punished for what. But not Princess Cleopatra." Senobastis smiled a little to herself. All curtsied or bowed very low and withdrew. Then she

90

said, "You must remember, both of you, only to do brave and silly things for something you want very, very much. You must remember that you were lucky this time, my Moon. Very lucky."

"Did you ever do a brave, silly thing, Mother?" asked Sun.

"Yes," said Cleopatra, and lifting her head, she laughed low, looking far out over the children. "Shall I tell you?"

"Yes," they both said, "tell us!"

"Well," said Cleopatra, "once upon a time when I was a girl, but a bigger girl than you, my Moon, I wanted very, very much to win a war. And the way to do it was to see the Roman general. I had to persuade him to take my side. But how was I to get to him? He was on the other side of the harbor, near the light-house, as a matter of fact. My enemies were between me and him."

91

"So what did you do, Mother?"

"You'll never guess. I had myself wrapped up in a carpet—a beautiful, soft carpet it was—and a friend of mine pretended to be a carpet-seller and took me across the harbor in a little boat. You know, my enemies might easily have sunk the boat or stopped him and taken me prisoner, or someone might have stepped on the carpet and broken my arm. But I was as lucky as you; it didn't happen. So my friend rowed me across and they pulled up the carpet—oh, that was dreadful, I was standing on my head!—and took it over to the Roman general and when he opened the carpet, there I was!"

"And did you make him take your side, Mother?"

"Oh, yes. It all went the way I meant it to. But it was silly and dangerous. Promise me, my Moon, you will always think very hard before you do anything silly and dangerous again."

Moon wriggled up onto the Queen's knee. "I promise, Mother," she said, "but next time can Sun and I go to the lighthouse when it is lighted up?"